STORIES FROM ESSEX

Edited By Jess Giaffreda

First published in Great Britain in 2019 by:

Young Writers
Remus House
Coltsfoot Drive
Peterborough
PE2 9BF
Telephone: 01733 890066
Website: www.youngwriters.co.uk

Book Design by Camilla Davis

SB ISBN 978-1-78988-239-1
Printed and bound in the UK by BookPrintingUK
Website: www.bookprintinguk.com
YB0396L

FOREWORD

Welcome, Reader!

Here at Young Writers our aim is to encourage creativity in children and to inspire a love of the written word. Each competition we create is tailored to the relevant age group, hopefully giving each child the inspiration and incentive to create their own piece of work, whether it's a poem or a short story. We truly believe that seeing their work in print gives pupils a sense of achievement and pride.

For Young Writers' latest nationwide competition, Spooky Sagas, we gave primary school pupils the task of tackling one of the oldest story-telling traditions: the ghost story. However, we added a twist – they had to write it as a mini saga, a story in just 100 words!

These pupils rose to the challenge magnificently and this resulting collection of spooky sagas will certainly give you the creeps! You may meet friendly ghosts or creepy clowns, or be taken on Halloween adventures to haunted mansions and ghostly graveyards!

So if you think you're ready... read on.

CONTENTS

Wells Park School, Lambourne End

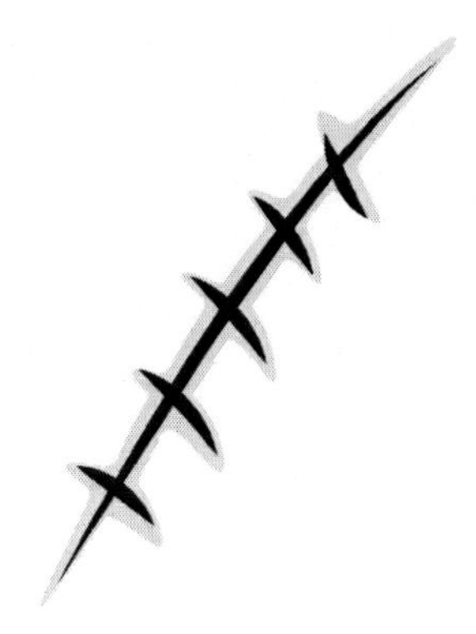

THE SPOOKY SAGAS

DARKNESS

In the dead of night, Lilly stealthily tiptoed towards the untouched trapdoor. She lifted the rusty handle and entered the darkness. The door slammed behind her. Lilly heard footsteps stumble across the floor. She froze in fear. All she could hear was a clock from upstairs.
Bang! Something fell from the ceiling, a ghostly shadow appeared at the end of the steps. The shadow moved towards Lilly.
"Hello?" she whispered. "Who's there?"
The figure slowly appeared through the darkness. It didn't look as scary as it did. She knew the monster.
"It's my dad! You're back! I missed you!"

Esmée Montague (9)
Boreham Primary School, Boreham

RETURN OF THE DEAD

It was the dead of night on Halloween and in the chilling attic, rats scampered around, afraid of what was lurking in the gloomy abyss. Hearing creaks in the rotting floorboards, Cheryl slumped out of bed and soon she would receive a creepy surprise. What was going on? Everything seemed so strange. As she was climbing up the attic staircase, shivers ran down her spine. Yeah, it was cold, we all knew that, but something wasn't quite right.
"Boo!" shouted the most hideous zombie ever!
"Arghh!" Cheryl screamed so loud, yet nobody came to help her.
"I've got you now!"

Harriet Rush (9)
Boreham Primary School, Boreham

MY EVIL NEIGHBOUR

It was a dark, stormy night and Owen unsteadily walked towards the tall, red house. He knocked on the door. *Thump! Thump! Thump!* Golden lights flickered behind curtains. Owen opened the door to find books, paper and dusty CDs scattered everywhere. Then all turned silent. The black shadow that he saw every evening at the window was now walking closer and closer. Her silence was frightening. Unsure of what would happen next, he turned around and ran for his life.
As nights went past, Owen saw her ugly shadow moving around in the window. Forever, he felt extraordinary fear.

Owen Ferguson (10)
Boreham Primary School, Boreham

THE HAUNTED HOUSE

Bob walked up to the house. His father had gone missing in its walls five weeks ago. Bob moved closer.
"*Arghh!*" a scream passed through the walls.
It sounded like his dad. He nervously moved nine steps closer. If he took one more, he would be inside. He had no choice! His father was in danger!
"*Arghh!*"
There it was again. Bob had no choice. He had to enter the house. Inside, he was chased by five guns, six knives and a candle with bright blue flames before he found it. His father's soul was being sucked out by Medusa!

Seán O'Brien (10)
Boreham Primary School, Boreham

A MYSTERIOUS HOUSE

Matt was trick or treating on Halloween. He knocked on the final, creepiest house. "Trick or treat?" he called.
There was an eerie silence. He thought of leaving when the door creaked open.
He went in and opened every door, no one was there. Then an eerie sound came from the basement. Matt stepped down the creaking steps, he crashed down the last two steps and gasped in horror. He saw a creepy ghost which suddenly disappeared. Matt turned and fled up the stairs and ran all the way home. He left his trick or treat bucket on the floor!

Joshua Little (9)
Boreham Primary School, Boreham

HAUNTED HALLWAYS

I was on the bus with my friend, Tyler, when I saw a haunted house. We shouted, "Stop the bus!"
We got our money back and went inside.
When we opened the door, lots of bats came fluttering out. Tyler saw some stairs so we went up them. Through the window, we saw a graveyard girl.
From the corner of my eye, I saw a lever so I said to Tyler, "Shall I pull that lever?"
Tyler said, "Yes!"
I pulled the lever and a set of stairs appeared. We went down them and a wrecking ball rolled towards us.

Noah Kenneth Ka Ming Fung (7)
Boreham Primary School, Boreham

THE SPOOKY GHOST AND CLOWN

Once upon a time, there was a little boy called Frank. He was lonely and one day, he saw a ghost and a clown with guns. He was walking down a dark forest on his own and he was nearly getting shot by a clown! Luckily, Frank didn't get hurt and lost the clown, but he saw a ghost. He was scared and furious! Suddenly, the ghost got the rest of the freaky ghosts and Frank screamed and shouted, "Go away!"
They finally went away. Frank found one of his parents and they lived happily and rich for life.

Jaylen Reggie Robinson Hawes (9)
Boreham Primary School, Boreham

THE ESSEX GHOST

It was the night before Halloween and all was still and serene. I saw a beautiful mist, blue and green, and out came a shadow that looked quite mean. Suddenly, I remembered it was from my bad dream! It stepped out of the mist and a ghostly figure stood before me, his eyes were black as coal. It looked like he was from history. He pointed at me and I could see he had something to ask me.
"Hey Maggie, do you like my outfit?"
"Yes," I said, "but it scared me a bit!"

Charlotte Hermitage (9)
Boreham Primary School, Boreham

TRAPPED!

Chloe opened her eyes. All she could see was pitch-black, even with her eyes wide open. She put her hands out but something was in the way. A drop of fear trickled down her spine while Chloe pushed as hard as she could against whatever was in front of her. She heard a click, then a creak, then whatever it was, it opened up. Chloe was astonished when she turned around to see what she was lying in. A tomb! Suddenly, Chloe heard a loud bang behind her. With her heart racing, she slowly turned around...

Maisie Lane (9)
Boreham Primary School, Boreham

THE OLD MURDERER

Once, I was on a bus and I saw a strange house, so I got off the bus and went inside. Everything was silent until I heard a footstep. It was getting closer and closer until I saw the face of an old lady with a piece of wood with nails hanging out of it.
Then she saw me so I ran and hid and she kept looking, saying, "Do you want to play hide-and-seek?"
Then she found me but I ran with her on my tail. I was running so fast, then I ran out!

Tyler Bolingbroke (7)
Boreham Primary School, Boreham

DARE DEVIL

There she was, standing in front of the most intimidating house in the world. She opened the door and she felt like she was in 'I'm A Celebrity... Get Me Out Of Here!'. There were spiders, flies and worst of all, snakes. Roxy hated snakes. She had been bitten by one when she was just four years old. She had been dared to do this so there was no going back. She stepped in and said, "Hello? Anyone here?" Sadly, there was an answer. It sounded like her mother. All of a sudden, she saw red, glowing eyes... She screamed!

Daisy Earnshaw-Gliddon (10)
Cann Hall Primary School, Clacton-On-Sea

THE HAUNTED GRAVEYARD

One dark night, Jack and Sarah were on an adventure in the spooky graveyard. They got cold and walked into the haunted house that they found. They heard whispering voices and stairs creaking. They came out. There came a loud scream from the other side of the graveyard. Sarah pulled out a mirror from her bag. They were monsters! They both ran home, monsters chasing them. They ran down a dark alleyway and more monsters followed. They got to a dead end, there was no way out. Monsters surrounded them, it was silent. Nothing else was heard...

Summer Gemma Warner (10)
Cann Hall Primary School, Clacton-On-Sea

A SHIVER RAN DOWN MY SPINE

I ran up the filthy path. I pushed the heavy door open and stepped inside. *Bang!* I looked behind and the door had shut. I tried to open it but it was locked. I looked around wearily. The wallpaper was torn and some of the floorboards were missing. What was my mum thinking when she said it was our new house? Not knowing what I was doing, I slowly started to walk up the stairs into a cold room. I saw empty boxes everywhere.
Suddenly, someone cackled behind me, "I've got you!" and a shiver ran down my spine...

Phoebe Pryor (10)
Cann Hall Primary School, Clacton-On-Sea

QUEEN OF THE NIGHT!

I began my journey home. It was freezing and pitch-black. Everything I heard was echoing in the darkness. Suddenly, I heard hooves clattering on the pavement. The noise got nearer and nearer. The trees shivered and leaves whistled in the wind. I saw two big, white horses pulling a big, black carriage. I was terrified, was this going to be the end? The carriage went right through me. I looked like the person in the carriage. I felt like I'd seen her before. It was Queen Victoria... My name is Victoria. Was it a ghost or a memory?

Mia Bell (10)
Cann Hall Primary School, Clacton-On-Sea

THE HORRIFIC HAUNTED HOUSE

I woke up on the floor in pitch-black. I couldn't remember what happened. *How am I here?* I stood up and looked around, only to see a note stuck on the wall, which was hard because the light wasn't on. I reached to the wall and felt the switch. I pressed it, which was a mistake. The wall opened to another room. Suddenly, something brushed past me. I touched my leg but nothing was there. I heard something approaching me. There I saw it. It was a wolf with beady eyes and its vile claws scratched me! I screamed!

Demi Daisy Toland (11)
Cann Hall Primary School, Clacton-On-Sea

THE GIRL WITH A BAT IN A HOUSE

One bitter night, a young girl woke up because she heard a noise. Then all of a sudden, a bat flew past her. She followed it into the basement.
After that, it turned into Dracula! She tried to run but he was too quick. As she backed away, she slammed her back into the wall. She was trapped, there was nowhere to run. Dracula was slowly coming towards her. When she tried to move, Dracula was there. She tried to scream but nothing came out. Dracula slowly sunk his teeth into her.
She woke up. It was just a dream!

Mila Vertigen (10)
Cann Hall Primary School, Clacton-On-Sea

THE SPOOKY HOUSE THAT TERRIFIED US

One Friday after school, me and my friend, Lana, decided to go into an abandoned, boarded-up house at the end of our street. It was dark and cold. No one had lived there for years. We started to hear voices and noises from upstairs. Doors began to bang. We thought it was haunted.
We then opened a door leading into the kitchen when my friends jumped out on us! They heard us talking about going there and thought they would scare us. That was the last time we went to the house. It was a day we'd never forget!

Libby Godfrey (10)
Cann Hall Primary School, Clacton-On-Sea

HIDE-AND-SEEK HORROR

He lay there in the cold, gloomy darkness of the cupboard under the stairs, which overflowed with spiders. He shivered at the thought of spiders and pictures of tarantulas filled his head. Slowly, his fear became bigger and bigger. Were they coming to find him or not? Then all of a sudden, the door burst open. *Creak!* Then when he looked, it was neither his brother or sister... it was a vampire! Was the vampire going to suck his blood and take him as a prisoner? No one knew, only he was never seen again!

Eloise Pettitt (10)
Cann Hall Primary School, Clacton-On-Sea

TRICK OR TREAT TERROR

It was on a dark Halloween night when my friend, Lola, and I went trick or treating. We knocked on some doors in a street we'd never been before. We knocked on the door of a creepy looking mansion. Then the door creaked and an old lady opened the door and filled our buckets up to the top.
When we walked away from the house, Lola's bucket was glowing. Then I finally plucked up the courage to empty her bucket. They were glow in the dark stones, not sweets! We couldn't stop laughing all the way home!

Hayley Gooch (11)
Cann Hall Primary School, Clacton-On-Sea

TOP HAT

We just got on the bridge and black fog emerged. Suddenly, there was a man with his eyelids and mouth stitched up. As we looked at him, he took his top hat off and the lights turned off. My brother quickly turned the lights back on and the man was gone.
After, we drove ahead for fifteen minutes in silence. My brother then told me about the story of the man who hanged himself on that bridge.
After he told me, I started to look around just in case. Then I realised the top hat was in the back seat...

Aiden Cornwell (10)
Cann Hall Primary School, Clacton-On-Sea

ZOMBIES AND SLIME

One day, my sister and I were walking in the woods. We came across a puddle that was filled with green, gooey, smelly slime. As we looked into the puddle, a very large zombie appeared with one eye. Then, more zombies came towards us! We ran and ran as fast as we could till we reached home.
As we reached home, they followed us and banged on the door till they knocked it down. We quickly ran upstairs and jumped into bed, hid under the covers and then we woke up. It was just a scary nightmare!

Jaimee Leigh Emma Botten (10)
Cann Hall Primary School, Clacton-On-Sea

THE HAUNTED HOUSE

Mum said, "Don't go to the haunted house!"
I never did until one day when my friends told me they were going and really wanted me to go, so I said I'd go as well.
When I went to the haunted house, my friends and I went in together. When we went in, the wallpaper was peeling off the walls. There were no lights. There was a weird chilling feeling. My friends had gone ahead so I ran ahead to them. I stopped and heard voices in the distance like whispers in my ears...

Konnie Faith Lyness (10)
Cann Hall Primary School, Clacton-On-Sea

IS IT A DREAM?

It was dark, so dark I could not see my hand when I held it to my face. I heard a whisper that seemed to spread through my whole body. A faint light appeared. I could see where I was! I was in a town square. It was deserted. I heard the whisper again. Out of the corner of my eye, I saw a dark figure appear. It began to approach me. As it got closer, the whispers got louder. It stretched its arm out to me...
I woke. As my eyes cleared, I saw the dark figure above me...

Erin Woodgate (10)
Cann Hall Primary School, Clacton-On-Sea

ALL WILL BE REVEALED...

"Mum, Dad, please let me live!"
"We're sorry."
7 years later...
Phil and Gabby heard the phone ring and after a lot of persuading and complaints from Gabby, Phil picked the phone up. "Hello?" He heard a familiar voice. A voice that was too familiar! It was Sofia, their daughter, their *dead* daughter! He dropped the phone on the now cold, hard floor. "S-s-s-ofia, Sofia's on the phone!"
Gabby picked up the phone and, still confused, listened to what Sofia had to say.
"All will be revealed. Just you wait, my murder story will come out!"

Amina Akhter (11)
Loxford School Of Science & Technology, Ilford

THE SLEEPOVER

The sky was blue and four girls were having a sleepover. They were telling spooky stories when one of the girls vanished. It was Ellie. The girls called her parents. "Ellie's missing!" They called the police. The officer said, "It's ghost traces!" The officer was right. They freaked out. Ghosts are real!
Suddenly, Tiffany and Molly disappeared. They heard a high-pitched scream through the mirror. Kelly felt a shock of fear running down her spine. She couldn't run away. She had to find her three friends. They had a full police investigation. What happened to her three friends?

Laiba Saleem (10)
Loxford School Of Science & Technology, Ilford

THE DEMIRAPTOR

I'm in an isolated road looking for help with my car. It's a moonlit, humid, foggy night and nobody is around.
"Hello? Anyone?"
I see this big, bell-like, dark shadow. Goosebumps take over me. I get closer to see and a smell of rotten animal fills the air.
"Oh, it's just a factory."
Squeaking noises come from inside. I start breathing heavily while walking to it. There's this warm breathing over my shoulder. I look back and a grey, hideous, open-chested, faceless creature is leaping towards me.
I say to myself, "Run and don't look back!"

Fahim Rangon Rahman (11)
Loxford School Of Science & Technology, Ilford

THE FIGURE

"Arghh!"
I fell down this unfamiliar tunnel into a room, a congested, eerie room. Daylight only poured in from a hole in the wall. *Where am I?* I had never seen this room in my grandma's house. Why did my parents have to go and celebrate their anniversary? This room gave me a spine-chilling feeling. However, then, a figure ambled behind me. I tried to speak but I was frozen with fear,
"H-hello," murmured the figure.
I quickly recognised the voice. As it approached nearer, I saw that it was my grandma!
"Tom, I finally found you! I was petrified!"

Mayra Farooq (11)
Loxford School Of Science & Technology, Ilford

HAIR-RAISING LIFT ADVENTURE!

"Holy macaroni!" I bellowed, searching my body as if I was under police interrogation. "Where are the house keys?" I desperately questioned.
With a swift spin, I headed towards the lift. Suddenly, the lift slithered and randomly made a stiff stop. The silence that followed was interrupted by eerie, faint whispers. Sweat poured uncontrollably from my palms. A scream attempted to arise from deep within me but failed. Fear had taken over my paralysed, fragile body. Figures circulated in my face. I was breathless as if the lift was closing in on me. The light flickered and I fainted...

Amana Nassor (11)
Loxford School Of Science & Technology, Ilford

DARE TO LIE

There was a girl called Maria. She lived with her parents. Maria had an alluring appearance, but she lied. Her parents cautioned her about the consequences.
One day, Maria's parents had to go away. Later, they left. The phone rang, Maria answered. Her parents asked Maria questions. She lied. Rapidly, the electricity went out. She started sobbing. She heard tapping. It happened again, but was now screeching! Maria fainted at the sound. A hooded figure appeared. It clutched Maria. She woke up and started hollering. Then the creature began pushing Maria into a wall. Only dust remained of the girl.

Javaria Bukht Hayat (11)
Loxford School Of Science & Technology, Ilford

THE ZOMBIES!

On the night of Halloween, there were three children, Johnny, Felix and Alex. The trio happened to be trick or treating. The trio all wore Grim Reaper costumes with masks and scythes. They all passed a graveyard with fresh graves in front of an old Halloween decorated house.
There came screams of "Brains! Ooh, brains!"
The trio got scared and Felix shouted, "Trick or treat?"
The two got angry at Felix and started to argue. While arguing, zombies came out of the graves. The trio squealed and ran away.
After all that, the zombies and graves were all fake!

Labib Alam (11)
Loxford School Of Science & Technology, Ilford

THE THING

Crash! Lightning struck an abandoned farmhouse. *Bang!* Eerily, something came out, but it wasn't human. Eleven-year-old Billy was alone in the village that night. He heard a knock at the door. Thinking it was his parents, he answered it. In the flash of the storm, he saw *The Thing!* He tried to shut the door but The Thing had made its way inside and tried to grab him with his grotesque hands. Billy fled, however fate caught up with him. The air was lethally toxic and his lungs filled up with the plague. He became the living dead...

Sami Ahmed (11)
Loxford School Of Science & Technology, Ilford

THE DEAL WITH THE DEVIL

In 1924, a twelve-year-old boy named Jason Jackson prayed to Satan and made a pact with the devil so that he could gain power.
A few days later, his body was taken over by strange essences. Nuns who came to assess his paranormal situation heard him speak a language which was in-between old English and ancient Latin. He was forced back by a sort of forcefield when he approached religious objects, his eyes would turn red.
Finally, two priests were brought for an exorcism. It took days until the devil's spirit was extracted out of him, its last howl.

Tahim Hossain (10)

Loxford School Of Science & Technology, Ilford

THE GRAVEYARD

Max was in the graveyard, visiting his father's grave. His father had died in a car crash. Max was driving the car when his father died. He saw his father's gravestone. *Here Lies Sam Parker - 1950-2018,* were the words engraved on the stone. Just then, he had a terrible flashback. He was about to leave but he saw a tall, dark figure lingering over him. He turned around to see a grotesque body. It was his *father!* Max dashed away.
He began to calm himself down. He told himself that it was just his imagination... or was it?

Adam Hanif (10)
Loxford School Of Science & Technology, Ilford

TRAPPED INDOORS

The floor creaked as poor Lily desperately wanted to escape. The creak made her heart leap like a frog and her pale fingers shake. Her feet were soon sore from tiptoeing and she had little chance of staying awake. The drowsy girl dragged herself along until her eyes widened as she saw a broad yet dingy passageway but her eyes caught her horrendous master's room lit and for that, Lily halted and decided to have a look. She turned stiff seeing a monster with a devilish smile and deep, piercing eyes as round as moons cleaning her jaws with blood...

Laiba Uddin (10)
Loxford School Of Science & Technology, Ilford

ETERNAL DARKNESS

I couldn't see anything, only the stars. Even though I was engulfed by the darkness, I could hear the movement of the worms and the raging winds howling like a grief-stricken mother mourning for her dead child.
Only twenty minutes ago, I was having so much fun with my friends at the carnival. The next thing I knew was that the creatures were chasing after me. Despite the situation I was in, I felt relieved as I knew that no more zombies were behind my back. I looked behind me. I saw a pair of eyes and they weren't human...

Rifah Alam (10)
Loxford School Of Science & Technology, Ilford

MAMA WILL FIND YOU...

My friends and I went to an abandoned school thinking we would all come back safely but I wasn't so fortunate...
We approached the abandoned school. My teeth chattered but I stopped it. We were in a classroom. Chairs and tables turned. No one cared. We chanted and a dark shadow ran past us. My breathing became fast. I closed my eyes. I heard footsteps. Everyone was gone. Then, no more.
I woke up tied to a table. The room was dark and all I ever saw were two purple eyes glistening in the dark night. I was caught.

Nageen Ahmadi (11)
Loxford School Of Science & Technology, Ilford

THE GIRL

My friends Rose and Marie and I went to a mansion. We were roaming around and spotted a box. Out of curiosity, we opened it and saw newspapers about a little missing girl. Just then, a cackling noise came. We saw a little girl with shards of glass in her body.
"Is that her?" I whispered.
She laughed, "You're right!" and disappeared out of our eyes.
We turned back and saw her presence. She took the piece of glass out of her eyes and mouth. I shrieked loudly, then my mum woke me up!

Sri Saanvi Vissapragada (10)
Loxford School Of Science & Technology, Ilford

THE TERRIFYING TEACHER

Boom! I heard a noise from the attic. I was upstairs in my room, texting on my phone. Miss Langson told me I should read a book when I got home.
As scared as I was, I went into the attic and saw Miss Langson. She looked horrendous, red liquid coming out of her swollen eyes, a white gown torn and a black hat over her tangled hair. Before she flew away, she handed me a book 'How To Live', and screamed, "Beware!"
The next day, everyone was wondering where she was, however, I knew...

Sara Jannat Ullah (11)
Loxford School Of Science & Technology, Ilford

THE MYSTERY

Max stepped off the bus and got into his house. He felt that there was something wrong, but he just couldn't quite put his finger on it. He walked around the house and turned the lights on. Well, he tried, but the lights just flickered. He ran into the bedroom and saw red eyes. He heard some petrifying sounds too. A green, slimy hand grabbed his shirt. Tension was written on his face. He scrambled and sprinted past the noises. He had escaped the grasp and hid in his room. He was safe, or was he...?

Aarit Parolia (10)
Loxford School Of Science & Technology, Ilford

THE GUARDIAN OF THE HOUSE

I walk upstairs to see a figure standing in the dark. I turn on the light but nobody's there. The growling sounds come closer. I turn around to see the most horrible creature!
I wake up to see a hole in the ceiling. I get a ladder and open a door to see a girl crying. I turn on my torch. She starts to laugh and crawls on the roof. My torch turns off. I tremble with fear, I can't move! She catches hold of me and drags me to a dark, cold corner. I hear tapping on the window...

Zahra Mujtaba (10)
Loxford School Of Science & Technology, Ilford

THE DARK FIGURE

I suddenly woke up in the middle of the night, feeling tired and hot. I wanted to turn the fan on but when I looked up to flip the switch, I saw the black figure of... a little girl. I could make out that she was standing, staring at me. I quivered. Even though the fan was just a foot away from my bed, I was so frightened that I couldn't turn it on. I had to sleep through the night feeling very hot.
When I woke up, I saw a suit on a stand. It wasn't a little girl.

Zaara Batcha (10)
Loxford School Of Science & Technology, Ilford

THE BASEMENT

One day, I was just watching a TV show but then Mum told me to fetch the laundry basket from the basement, so I did as I was told.
As I was walking down, I caught a glimpse of a stick-thin figure in the shadows. I was petrified! I was afraid to even move! I slowly reached for the light switch. I was so relieved that it was just a lamp... but that didn't explain the screams I heard...

Jasmine Matharu (10)
Loxford School Of Science & Technology, Ilford

THE SCARY NIGHT

Jim was lost in the caliginous night with no shelter. He perambulated a few feet forward and found a primordial, wrecked house. Surprisingly, the door was open. He stepped inside. Cobwebs were visible. Creepily, the door shut on itself... He was locked in. A candle was glowing and a message was written on the wall in blood: 'Hello Jim'.

"Happy Halloween!" a voice cried out.

It was Jim's dad.

"Do you like the decorations?"

"Yes!" said Jim. "You really creeped me out!"

"Yes, they're really scary!" Jim's dad said. "Let's have a party!"

"Let's get the party started!" Jim exclaimed.

Maximilien Pitton (9)
Loyola Preparatory School, Buckhurst Hill

THE HAUNTED HOUSE

Ben saw the abandoned, haunted house and went inside. Vampires ambled around the graveyard and zombies popped up from their gravestones, scaring the life out of him! Inside the house, it was one fright after the other. White ghosts emerged from nowhere and skeletons' bones creaked loudly. The things that frightened him the most were the sinister figures that were perambulating around. Suddenly, a cupboard creaked open and he suddenly heard ghostly voices all around him. The voices screamed, "Woo!"
Ben became so scared that he ran away into the eerie night, screaming with fear until he got home.

Paul Murphy (9)
Loyola Preparatory School, Buckhurst Hill

TRICK OR TREATING

Halloween night; an eerie evening. The only light radiated from pumpkins whose pungent aroma filled the air from the candle-burnt flesh inside. A ghostly gang of misfits perambulated across the caliginous streets like a band of brothers on an epic adventure. A ghost, a scarecrow, a mummy and a vampire.
"Hey, who are you?" shrieked Harry the scarecrow.
"We are not alone!"
Terrified, they slowly turned to face the ominous figure dressed only in a cloak and a bowler hat. Spine-chillingly, the figure floated into the night sky like a balloon. Was this an illusion or was it real?

Cillian Gowers (10)
Loyola Preparatory School, Buckhurst Hill

THE HAUNTED CAVE

It was a thunderous night. Rain was gushing down full of fury, quicker than light, while eerie sounds of bats made babies cry. Everything was perilous, detrimental and caliginous! An ambitious boy called Fred thought this weather was perfect to explore.
Nearby was a haunted cave that was cursed. Fred slowly got closer and closer and then he went inside the grey cave. Bats were howling louder than lions. In the distance was a pernicious vampire!
Shoot! Out of his mouth came sticky cement! Fred ran faster than Usain Bolt and phew, he escaped!
"I am never exploring again!"

Aditya Singh (9)
Loyola Preparatory School, Buckhurst Hill

TRANSYLVANIA ADVENTURE

Bleak clouds covered the sky, it was as if a death sentence was calling on Transylvania. A loquacious boy named Zareb had been lurking around the rural, isolated town. This boy could hear enigmatic and peculiar noises from the castle. Bats with coal-black wings fluttered aggressively which enthralled him. Rapturous rain roared down as Zareb entered the desolate castle. Shadows of vampires cast on the moonlit floor and rose up above him. Vigorously, the leader bit into his neck which made crimson blood gush out like a fountain. Zareb had metamorphized into a repugnant, pernicious and petrifying vampire.

Zareb Rizvi (10)

Loyola Preparatory School, Buckhurst Hill

THE FOOTSTEPS

The sky was jet-black as stars illuminated the night. It was as windy as a storm or hurricane. Every single person was in their house. It was Halloween but nobody went trick or treating. Unfortunately, this man named Chris ignored that and went to the graveyard. He was cautious where he laid down his steps. He finally arrived at his dead father.
He started praying but in the middle of this, he heard someone saying, "I'm coming for you!" Nobody else was there. Chris was fossilised. He concluded what he was doing, got in his car and drove off...

Mikhail Safin Hussain (10)
Loyola Preparatory School, Buckhurst Hill

THE MONSTER SURPRISE!

It was a dark, caliginous, stormy night. The muddy field was very quiet and a cold breeze blew. Alex was walking home from detention. His black hair was soaking from the lashing rain. He stared up at the hill and spotted an abandoned house that he was oblivious to before. Suddenly, he heard rustling in the bushes and something growled. He sprinted towards the house to escape. The door was jammed, he was cornered! The creature pounced! Alex was shocked and fell.
He looked up and he realised it was his cute little puppy with a stick in its mouth!

Adam Tsang (10)
Loyola Preparatory School, Buckhurst Hill

UNLIKELY FRIENDS - TIM AND JERRY

Tim loved action. On one skydiving trip, he was abruptly thrown out before he was ready. His chute wouldn't open. Panic ensued as he thought about his imminent death. Suddenly, he felt cold hands grabbing onto his waist and he began to slow down from his descent. Tim passed out.

When he awoke, he was on top of Mount Everest and inside an ancient, spooky castle. Before him, a ghost appeared. He called himself Jerry. Tim knew he was a ghost so he was both terrified and grateful at the same time, as he knew Jerry had saved his life.

Leonardo Tran (9)
Loyola Preparatory School, Buckhurst Hill

THE HAUNTED HOUSE

It was gloomy and it was thundering rapidly and you could hear horrifying wolf sounds. There was a boy just the age of ten and there was nobody with him. He was a trick-or-treater. He went to the door to get candy. It looked haunted as it was hair-raising and blood-curdling. The door opened, he was petrified but he was curious so slowly, he went in but the door slammed shut! His heart stopped! He could hear whispers. He tried shouting, no one answered.
Then the light came on and he ran out the door, rapidly and swiftly.

Arty Clarkin (10)
Loyola Preparatory School, Buckhurst Hill

THE BLACK FIGURE

One night, thunder woke me up. It was
midnight but I was thirsty so I slowly crept
downstairs.
When I got to the kitchen, it was dark and
thunder struck. I couldn't find the lights so I got
a drink in the dark. Then a figure appeared
that I could hardly see. It started following me.
I dashed out of the room as fast as I could,
spilling my drink all over me. It was freezing but
I just ran. Then I was trapped!
In the corner, I noticed it was my dad.
He said, "Why are you awake?"

Daniel Halcrow (9)
Loyola Preparatory School, Buckhurst Hill

THE BAD CREATURE

As I slept, a noise woke me, an eerie, preternatural noise.
Outside, the moon was up and it was pitch-black. Suddenly, a pair of bloodshot eyes and razor-sharp teeth glanced at me. I was so petrified that I could've run away screaming but I didn't, I just kept still. As he was going to devour me, he choked and gurgled until he fell on the rusty ground. This creature was dead. Then I saw a keen dagger with a fatal type of acid pouring out of it. I wonder who killed this beast. Was it a hero?

Maximilian Huang (9)
Loyola Preparatory School, Buckhurst Hill

THE DOLL

In a gloomy, sinister house, John woke up in an old, pitch-black room with spiders and cobwebs hanging from the ceiling. John heard pounding footsteps in the attic and a whispering voice urging him to come up. John noticed a door with a dusty knob, he turned the handle that led to a ladder. He saw a switch and pulled it and was shocked by the bright light. He slowly crept down and saw an eerie doll. The light switched on and off as if it was broken. The doll had moved to the door. John left rapidly...

Ciaran Brett (10)
Loyola Preparatory School, Buckhurst Hill

THE VAMPIRE

It was a dark, caliginous and stormy night. Thunder growled, lightning crackled, rain poured out of the sky and wind howled like a victim.
"Where am I?"
I was in a dark room with a tiny window. I opened my eyes more. I squinted to see it but huddled in a dark corner, there was a shadowy figure clothed in a black cloak. I opened my mouth to say something but nothing came out. I lingered closer and pulled off the cloak. It was just a chair, covered in a black cloak!

Oliver Morgan (9)
Loyola Preparatory School, Buckhurst Hill

THE CREEPY HOUSE THAT MAKES YOU RUN AWAY

It was a dark, scary night and there wasn't a single gloomy star in the sky.
There were scary, petrifying skeletons that whispered, "Never come in this haunted, black house, otherwise you will get killed by the horrible, gigantic vampire!"
Suddenly, the door creaked open. Slowly, I stepped in. There was a horrifying trap on me. Then an enormous, terrifying vampire appeared and was about to suck my blood but I killed him with a sword! Suddenly, a haunted monster appeared... I walked through the dark, dismal corridor and stumbled upon the master's bedroom. I heard a creepy cackle...

Laiba Mehmood (8)
Redbridge Primary School, Redbridge

THE WEIRDEST HALLOWEEN!

One cold evening, Shania was skipping down the road. She passed an eerie, old house. Maybe her bucket of sweets could do with some more? Eagerly, Shania knocked on the black door. Something flew from the shattered house and pulled her inside. She felt jittery all over.
It said, "Sorry for taking you through the window!"
Then the figure stepped into the light. It was a witch! Shania backed away carefully.
"I am not bad," it said, "my mum is!"
We shook hands and went on a crazy broomstick ride. Shania wondered, could she ever become friends with this witch?

Samaira Ayub (9)
Redbridge Primary School, Redbridge

LIGHTS OUT!

It was nearly pitch-black and I started to get tired.
Ghosts circled me and whispered, "It's coming for you!"
I thought to myself, *what's coming for me?* I burned with nervousness. The lights flickered. The door creaked open. A cold shiver ran up my spine. Suddenly, I heard a loud crash and scream that nearly broke my eardrums. I followed to where I heard it. I entered this large door. The door slammed shut. Then something grabbed me and pulled me into the darkness. It tried to penetrate with one of its fangs. I kicked out with all my might...

Lut Rifan (9)
Redbridge Primary School, Redbridge

THE MYSTERY OF THE MAN WITH A TWISTING HEAD

On a cold winter's night, a humble fourteen-year-old boy visited his trustworthy friend's house. He was striding to his warm house, wanting a great tasty dinner. Just then, a man with gleaming red eyes pointed at him. Then he held out a sharp silver knife! He charged at the young boy!
"Arghh!" screamed the helpless boy.
After that the dreadful ugly man twisted his head like a creepy owl searching for its tasty prey! Luckily, the poor, frightened boy dodged the sharp knife. Just then the psycho man pulled out some grenades! Oh no, what would he do now?

Shayaan Islam (8)
Redbridge Primary School, Redbridge

THE FORBIDDEN SHADOW

It was the dead of night. Bright, gleaming moonlight loomed across the land. The tall, towering trees whispered mean things to me. Fear surrounded me as I stepped closer to my doom. My sweaty hands reached towards the door. I found myself meandering through a narrow, dark, dismal corridor. I approached a fairly large room. Suddenly, I heard a big bang. I was trapped in that horrendous, spine-chilling room. It was infested with hairy rats. The sickening stench of rotten bodies filled my nose. Then a deafening cackle broke the silence. A face as pale as death stared at me...

Siddra Ahmed (9)
Redbridge Primary School, Redbridge

THE UNDERWORLD

One spooky night, there lived a ghost called Lilly. She lived in the underworld with her best friend, Milly.
The next night, she accidentally came out her grave while sleeping.
When she woke up, she was lying on some grass. Lilly looked down, her eyes widened like an orange. Looking around, she tried to find her grave but she couldn't until she saw houses in the distance. She flew towards them and thought, *this isn't a graveyard!* She knew she was lost but she thought she could settle in.
A few minutes later, she felt weird and started dreaming...

Harleen Karir (8)
Redbridge Primary School, Redbridge

SPOOKVILLE!

James was having a picnic in the park, he was enjoying his stinky cheese sandwich in the sunset when suddenly he heard a voice coming from the bushes. "Come, my dear, I have something to show you!" He thought it was his mum so he followed the voice. He went through the prickly bushes, under the diagonal trees and into a dark alleyway. It led him to Spookville! He could see zombies, skeletons, bats and vampires everywhere. A shiver went down his spine. A zombie came up to him and exclaimed, "Trick or treat?" James then realised it was Halloween!

Eliza Fatimah Syeda (8)

Redbridge Primary School, Redbridge

THE MONSTER CURSE

Jake was a boy who loved exploring. One day, he made a mistake! He went to the ancient temple where people got murdered long ago. Jake found a gem there and accidentally broke it! Out came a slithering serpent... it had so many spikes and had arms.

Jake asked the monster, "Who are you?"

He replied, "I am Serpent!"

Jake was running to get the gem and luckily got it and faced it at the monster. It was scared! He promised that he'd never hurt beings again. The monster finally found animal friends and lived happily ever after.

Rison Sanjul Kathiresan (8)
Redbridge Primary School, Redbridge

ORPHAN KID

There was a girl named Cheryl, aged seven. She
was an orphan, her mum and dad died.
She went into a forest. In it, she heard wolves
howling and witches cackling. It was a dark,
stormy night when she came.
As she was in the screaming, panic-stricken
forest, she saw a head rolling away into the
darkness. She screamed but nothing came out.
Cheryl ran after it but she struggled in her
black rags.
The head was on a body and the person asked,
"Can I eat you?"
Cheryl didn't answer, she screamed and ran!
Cheryl never ever came back...

Sasha Chohan (8)
Redbridge Primary School, Redbridge

I NEED A CODE!

I went to explore my attic. I saw an old, dusty radio. There were bottles of wine littered in the attic. There was a spell in the bottle. I read it out loud. Suddenly, the door closed. A ghost with googly eyes appeared, his teeth were as sharp as knives, ready to kill!

It spoke, "Give me a code!"

"Which code?" I said, shaking.

I remembered I saw a code on the sturdy ladder.

"5896!" I shouted. He was thinking, how could I have known it?

I would never go in that dreadful attic again, I felt scared witless!

Aanya Shah (8)

Redbridge Primary School, Redbridge

LOCKED IN A DREAM

On a cold, windy, snowy day, a foggy mist covered a house. In that house, two girls were having a sleepover. One of them got stuck in their dream! The girl's name was Joan. She was in a pitch-black room in her dream. She was panic-stricken and surrounded by mist.
A mist spoke, "Beware, go! Go away forever!"
Then she found a door. It creaked open. She took one step, just like when NASA's first ship landed on the moon.
"Oh no!" she said.
The light hovered over her. The light came from the room, oh no...

Nashid Nur (8)
Redbridge Primary School, Redbridge

THE GHOST'S DELIGHT

As I stumbled into the dark forest, I came across a hospital. *I love exploring so I'm going in.*
"Wait, what type of hospital is this?"
All of a sudden, I heard eerie sounds. I found out it was a mental hospital!
"Get out!" it screamed as it tried to possess me.
I ran and ran, it was there. I screamed. I had to kill it!
"I see you," it whispered.
I found matchsticks. I lit them up and burned it alive! Just then, a shadow lurked in the dark. I jumped, it just touched my back... oh no!

Abida Choudhury (9)
Redbridge Primary School, Redbridge

THE NARROW, BLACK ALLEY

One day, a girl named Jasmine was at a fair
eating some tasty ice cream.
She then asked her parents if she could go and
have a walk and they replied, "Yes, but be back
soon!"
So off she went, down a narrow, black alley.
Her parents actually thought she was walking
to a ride but they were wrong...
After an hour, they didn't know where she was.
Jasmine was walking past an aisle of homeless
men. She had salty sweat across her forehead
as they grinned. She then came to something
that suddenly grabbed her and whizzed away...

Fatima Shah (8)
Redbridge Primary School, Redbridge

THE WICKED KING AND THE WOLF

Once upon a land of misery, the king sent darkness upon the land. The first person that was an outsider to discover the land was an officer, Max. He investigated. When he met some of the people that lived there, they told Max about the king. Max travelled through the dark, gloomy forest to the king's castle.
The door was unlocked, like he was expecting him. Suddenly, he heard a vicious growl. He was being chased by a human-like wolf. Then, the king's guards blocked his path and the wolf gobbled him up like he was a tiny chicken.

Nabid Ali (8)
Redbridge Primary School, Redbridge

THREE MYSTERY MURDERS

I lay down, covering myself with a blanket of leaves. They were coming. I could hear approaching footsteps. The bunch of dead bodies covered my view of the murderers. They were coming for me! What did they want? I rolled and rolled until I could see three tall figures with torches. Rumours were spreading very fast about murderers who come out at midnight. Unluckily, I was there with the murderers and they were searching for me.
As I rolled across the field of leaves, I came across a gate with blood dripping from it. What could be behind it?

Rianna Safiyah Ali (9)
Redbridge Primary School, Redbridge

THE HOUSE OF HORROR

It was a dark and gloomy night, there wasn't a single shining star in sight.
The howling of the wind whispered quietly, "Stay away!"
In the distance, I heard a hungry beast howling. I cautiously opened the door. As I walked closer and closer, I could see red, bloody footsteps. I then walked into a dark room full of stuff. In the darkness, something moved closer and closer. I opened a prickly, wooden cupboard. Suddenly, something pushed me! It then jumped on me. I reached a sword from a display and hit it on his neck.

Hamza Hassan (9)
Redbridge Primary School, Redbridge

THE DREADED HOUSE!

Suddenly, far away in the distance, I saw a haunted house. The house had passwords on the door. I pointed at one of the passwords, the door swung open. I stumbled upon the kitchen. The fridge moved forward. I didn't dare to touch it. I knew something fishy was going on. I entered the washroom, it had damp all over the wall. I entered the master bedroom and saw eyeballs on show. I realised there was a witch above me.
She crackled and said, "How dare you enter my house!" and she vanished.
I ran out and never came back.

Kashvi Kirthi (8)
Redbridge Primary School, Redbridge

TRAPPED IN THE WITCH'S SPELL

Apparently, I ended up in a blood-curdling forest. I felt alarmed. The howling of the wind warned me of danger ahead. I could hear the deafening screams of the witch. I heard a noise which distracted my attention. I turned to see what it was. It was a bloodthirsty witch! Suddenly, the sinister witch trapped me in one of her spells. *What shall I do?* All of a sudden, I saw the magic blue owl which breaks witch's spells. I screamed for help. The sparkle from the owl's emerald, deep green eyes broke the spell. I cried with joy.

Aarna Patel (9)
Redbridge Primary School, Redbridge

HERE TODAY, GONE TOMORROW

First, I was in my bedroom and now I was here. The bitter taste of dirt filled my mouth as the wind pushed me. The smell of damp leaves and raw sewage filled the air. Despite the smell, this reminded me of where Dad died. I was crestfallen and miserable. As I stepped on the ramshackle, wooden porch, the crows cried as loud as a drum. Immediately, a black shadow dashed behind me.
Squelch! I stepped into a bloody puddle.
"Emily," someone mumbled my name.
Dad was here and I knew it, that voice was so similar!

Raisa Kabir Khan (9)
Redbridge Primary School, Redbridge

THE FOREST

As I stepped into the pitch-black forest, a strange, gloomy light shone out of a tiny crevice through the gigantic trees. Suddenly, a black dash flew off a tree.

"Is anyone there?" I questioned.

I was motionless. The moon rose. I knew I needed to go home but couldn't. A hideous face was placed in front of me. Blood as red as an apple poured out of its large mouth. I stood there, paralysed in fear. Instantly, the creature bit into my arm. I felt as if I was going to die. Then, I suddenly collapsed on the firm ground.

Kaeshikan Pratheepan (9)
Redbridge Primary School, Redbridge

THE HOUSE OF NIGHTMARES!

Lightning struck and the moon shone upon a rusty, ancient house. The wind howled in circles around me. Red, scorching eyes reflected on the path. Figures crowded me and seemed to fall asleep. The door creaked open. I crept into a room that had a sign saying: *Beware!* There were gooey eyeballs on the counter and dead bodies getting cooked up. Spiders surrounded me and I went into the fridge.
"Monsters!" I yelled.
I grabbed some brains and garlic and the monsters ate them. I saw a snake and used it to get out.

Hana Faruqi (8)
Redbridge Primary School, Redbridge

THE HAUNTED HALLWAY

Gordie got lost in the woods. She came across an abandoned house. She decided to go in.
As she went in, she swallowed dust and her foot got stuck. She got up and went in the bathroom. She saw slimy eyeballs and bloody handprints on the wall! She freaked out. She wanted to leave.
Suddenly, the door locked. Gordie saw bloody puddles. A spirit dragged her into the drain but she saw a pipe and hit it. She ran to unlock the door, she could hear its ugly scream echoing through the haunted hallway. She ran and never looked back...

Maryam Choudhury (8)
Redbridge Primary School, Redbridge

THE HAUNTED HOUSE

It was a gloomy, pitch-black night. I could hear thunder. It was all calm and quiet.
Sticky spiderwebs were covering the outside of the abandoned house. All of a sudden, a glass window shattered onto the floor. The wind went past me and warned, 'Beware, don't come in!'
I could taste bitter rat hair flying into my mouth. White, pale stars were shining brightly. I was nervous. I saw dead bodies on the floor. There were sinister tall trees. In the blink of an eye, the huge black door creaked open. Sweat dripped...

Hannah Javaid (9)
Redbridge Primary School, Redbridge

THE HOUSE THAT NOBODY KNOWS!

It was a dark, gloomy night and the majestic sky split into half as the moon was rising. I felt I was in a nightmare! In an instant, the fragile window shattered into thousands of tiny pieces like a glass blizzard. Suddenly, the door creaked open. As I cautiously approached the door, I thought to myself, *should I go inside?* In front of me, there was a door. I was shaking! Suddenly, eyeballs came alive. I felt paralysed with fear. I picked up a stick and threw it when the eyeballs weren't looking and ran out.

Mahnoor Faisal (8)
Redbridge Primary School, Redbridge

HALLOWEEN TOWN!

One day, a boy called Tom was on the beach
with his family. He thought he heard his mum
call his name. He followed the voice. It led him
to an unknown place called Halloween Town.
He nearly had a heart attack!
Crystal-white slime oozed out of the walls,
lightning hit down. There were monsters
everywhere! Would this be the end of him? He
just saw a vampire go towards him. He realised
it was his mum! Instead, she sucked blood from
his veins. He then turned into a vampire, living
the life with creepy, freaky, filthy monsters!

Jannah Ahmed (9)
Redbridge Primary School, Redbridge

THE HOUSE

The sky turned pitch-black as I entered the eerie dungeon. As I went in, I felt as if someone was grabbing my neck. I ran and ran to find a kitchen knife. I ran back to find a hideous, tranquil monster staring at me, barking, "Who are you? Get out!"
I ran to him and attempted to stab him. I screamed as loud as a bomb but no one was bound to listen.
As I closed my eyes and opened them, more people gathered around.
"Wake up!" came a screechy voice.
Perhaps it was a freaky dream after all...

Muhammad Khawaja (8)
Redbridge Primary School, Redbridge

HOUSE OF HORRORS

It was a dark, gloomy night. The wolves howled in the distance. The bright full moon lit up the sky. The wind whistled. Suddenly, the odour of rotten flesh led me to a haunted house behind the forest. The door creaked open. I walked in. The smell of rotten egg filled the air.
All of a sudden, some ghosts circled me. I screamed. I ran around lots of corners until I reached a door that warned: *Highly Poisonous Snakes!*
That was when I got an idea. I would trap the ghost in the room, and that was what I did.

Ashna Vijayan (8)
Redbridge Primary School, Redbridge

STUCK IN A HOUSE FULL OF DEATH!

As I stepped in the ramshackle house, my heart dropped with fear. I never had thought I would have been in such a terrifying scene. Suddenly, I heard footsteps coming towards me. Shivers ran down my spine. As quick as a flash, a black figure dashed across the room. I felt like a knife was twisting through my flesh.
In the distance, the glass shattered, causing the glass to fall on the floor. I took three steps forward and the door slammed shut. I tried to open it but it was locked. In front of my eyes, I froze still...

Maisha Baloch (9)
Redbridge Primary School, Redbridge

THE KIDNAP

Terrified screams echoed loudly in my ears as the wretched haunted house stood in front of me. Frightened, I grabbed the dusty, old handle and entered. Petrified, I stumbled along the pitch-black corridor and paused. I heard crying in my ears. Suddenly, I saw a figure rapidly running in circles many times. Afraid, I entered a random room and hid under the bed.
A few minutes later, the figure entered the room.
What am I going to do now? I should just hope for the best, why did I do this? I miss home!

Ayyan Hossain (8)
Redbridge Primary School, Redbridge

STUCK IN THE HAUNTED HOUSE!

It was the dead of night. I suddenly felt an instant cold. Three ghosts appeared and surrounded me. I got terrified and ran into a dark house. I ended up in a rotten bathroom. The bathtub was also rotten. The water was very dirty. There was a big door near the bathtub.
As I entered the room, I could see darkness. Where was the switch? I felt a string. As I pulled it, everything became bright. Three ghosts surrounded the room and locked me in. *What shall I do now? How do I get out? Will I be stuck here?*

Asviha Rajakumar (9)
Redbridge Primary School, Redbridge

THE HAUNTED HOUSE

It was dark and my friends asked if we could go out.
I responded, "Yes!"
We went out and played a game, truth or dare. My friends picked me to go in the haunted house. I yelled no but they insisted if I didn't go, they wouldn't be my friends. I did it. I went inside, there were dead bodies, it was scary! Suddenly, I heard a voiceless ghost. The room was full of spiders. It was terrifying! I went into the room, there was a trapdoor opened. I fell inside. I was dizzy! I collapsed and fainted...

Allison Jacome (9)
Redbridge Primary School, Redbridge

HOUSE NUMBER 13

It was a noisy night and all the night animals were howling and growling like mad. The hissing wind spread right across my ear, whispering, "Beware! Beware!"
Sometimes I felt like I was being followed. Witches cackled. Wolves barked and there were other monstrous sounds.
Moments later, before my eyes was a huge, ginormous mansion. Cold sweat trickled down my back as I could smell a dead body being mixed in stew. Slowly, I crept through the door and I saw something that looked like a kitchen...

Myesha Hossain (8)
Redbridge Primary School, Redbridge

THE HOUSE OF SUDDEN DEATH

It was a dark, mysterious night. It was rainy so I decided to go in the house. The wind was howling, "Get away!"
Suddenly, the windows cracked into a trillion pieces. I walked in. The trees bent towards me. I was scared! I heard a loud bang from upstairs. I was curious so I went upstairs. I saw several rooms so I went in the biggest one, the master bedroom. It had a vampire on the sofa. I touched it and it came alive and chased me! I couldn't move. I was stuck, so I bit the vampire's hand.

Aaron Lachani (8)
Redbridge Primary School, Redbridge

THE HAUNTED HOUSE

As I walked into the abandoned house, I felt a shiver up my spine. Now I am walking to the creaking, wooden house. I took one look at the old house. There was brutal damage everywhere! I'm feeling flabbergasted. There was only one way to go, the old stairs. Every step makes a creaking sound.
As I reached the stairs, an awkward vampire saw me. I ran as quick as I could. He was as fast as a cheetah! Now I was going to face the figure. I caught the awkward figure and locked him in. Would the door open?

Asvin Sureshkumar (8)
Redbridge Primary School, Redbridge

THE OUTBREAK!

It was a dark, gloomy night. Rain was pouring. Suddenly the house door creaked open. I went through, goo going on my foot. The door slammed. I went up the stairs and fell in a moonlit, sinister, deep trapdoor. Something was coming. It was flesh-hungry zombies. I jumped and found a hatch. I went through it. It led to the master bedroom. Suddenly a zombie giant came. I went through the legs and got a gun. I shot it and it died.
Then it came back to life. I got my backpack, escaped and I ran away quickly!

Nathen Virdee (8)
Redbridge Primary School, Redbridge

MIDNIGHT STRIKES

It was a dark, gloomy night and not a single star was to be seen. In the distance, I could see a house. It looked abandoned. I checked the time. It was midnight and everybody knows this legend, if you are near an abandoned house at midnight, you get haunted. I was curious. I entered the house and heard a ghostly groan. Something touched my back, my face turned ashen. At first, I thought the legend was fake but it was real. I was actually getting haunted! I was horrified! The doors had closed. I was stuck!

Liza Khan (9)
Redbridge Primary School, Redbridge

FROM BREATH TO DEATH!

It was a dark, misty night and not a single sound could be heard.
The wind howled and swooped past me, it said, "Beware, beware! Turn away now!"
That didn't scare me. I started to sweat and my face got hot. The wind howled in a cylinder around me as I walked to the front door and pushed it open. I walked up the stairs and opened the door to the master bedroom. I walked around and it was charcoal-black. I saw a clown. In the corner, I saw a cupboard. I pushed the clown and ran...

Simrit Kaur Sahote (9)
Redbridge Primary School, Redbridge

THE SPOOKY OLD HAUNTED HOUSE

As I was walking in the forest in the middle of the night, I saw a haunted house that was spooky. I went on the doorstep but I didn't go inside the haunted house. I was frightened because the house was creepy.
I went inside the haunted house. When I opened the dull, old door, it was broken. I was panic-stricken but when I went into the house, I saw a boy running upstairs! I was shocked that a boy was in the house!
I went to check upstairs and heard the boy call out... it was Tom!

Aliyah Hussain (8)
Redbridge Primary School, Redbridge

THE TEMPLE

Once, there was a boy named Tom Peterson. He was exploring a forbidden temple. He was tired and so sat down for a rest. It was dark and quiet. Suddenly, skeleton arms were grabbing him from behind. Tom tried not to scream. He kicked the arms and was trying to escape. Immediately, he could see there was a small shadow approaching, it was getting closer! As it emerged from the shadows, Tom realised the figure was wearing a stone crown, shining armour and torn cape. It was the skeleton king...

Aidan Wan (9)
Redbridge Primary School, Redbridge

THE HOUSE WITH NO NAME

It was midnight. There, in the darkness, was a big, abandoned house. There were gargoyles holding axes bigger than woodcutters. Then I went inside. At the corner of my eye, I could see the bathroom. I went in. I could see the wallpaper peeling off. I just went to the next room. There was the most disgusting thing I'd ever seen in my life! I was so disgusted that I went to the next room. I saw someone coming. I grabbed a knife, then I stabbed it. Then I ran away and never looked back...

Sreen Peruboina (8)
Redbridge Primary School, Redbridge

HAUNTED HOUSE

I crept slowly into the house and saw a big centipede on the floor laying its slime everywhere like a trail of icky slime. I heard moving around upstairs and saw an ugly witch looking at me face-to-face. I suddenly stopped looking at her and I focused on the problem in the house. I ran as fast as I could because there was a huge bang. Noises coming from upstairs. All the doors were locked and I couldn't escape but the window was open. It was at the top of the house, so I got a rope...

Isra Hussain (8)

Redbridge Primary School, Redbridge

FORBIDDEN FOREST

A girl lived near a forest with her mother in a little cottage, her name was Mandy, she was ten years old.
One day, while Mandy was coming back from school, she saw a path leading into the forbidden forest. Mandy kept thinking, *should I go in or not?* She followed the narrow path. Finally, she got to a cave.
Inside was pitch-black. Many could see a figure in the beam of light.
When she came out of the cave, she saw a rock, it said: 'Beware! Beware! Do not pass!'

Khadija Miah (9)
Redbridge Primary School, Redbridge

A MYSTERY MEETING!

I was asleep when I heard a pair of voices walking towards me. I jumped into my cupboard. I fell backwards and the back of my cupboard opened. I ran inside this mysterious opening. I ran to the right and kept on running onwards but a moving figure in the distance stopped me. I got out my torch.
Then, when the beam of light shone onto my uncle, I exclaimed, "What are you doing here, Bert?"
I tried to whisper but no reply came back so I solemnly gave a small moan.

Hafsa Yousaf (8)
Redbridge Primary School, Redbridge

THE GRAVEYARD

It was nearly the dead of night. I went into the spooky graveyard. I was surrounded by gravestones. I was frightened. Once I was in, the ground broke and I tripped over one of the pieces and then found the others. I put it together, the ground started shaking. I wobbled and fell down. It shook harder and harder, then I fell on my back. The ground stopped. I got up, figures emerged from the ground. I was gasping for my breath. I stared at them, they stared at me, I was frightened...

Leo Evangelou (9)
Redbridge Primary School, Redbridge

HELL OF ZOMBIES!

It was a dark, gloomy night and I was all alone.
In the distance, I could make out a house. I slowly crept towards it.
As I got closer, the wind whispered, "Stay away!"
The house looked terrifying with bats all over.
As I pushed the door open, three mobs all attacked me at once. They were zombies, a witch and a spider. As quick as a flash, I took out a penknife and quickly stabbed all of them to death. Today was the worst and most horrible day of my whole life!

Aiden Cleaves (8)
Redbridge Primary School, Redbridge

THE ATTIC OF HELL - STUCK WITH GHOSTS

I opened my eyes, not knowing where I was. The last thing I remembered was me looking for every potential hiding spot to get away but I bumped my head and dozed off. The room was lit by candlelight. I could make out that I was in the attic. Suddenly, a wooden bucket fell and I turned around to see a gruesome, fat figure lingering over me. It beckoned for vampires and more ghosts holding daggers! I awoke, squirming in my bed, relieved that none of it was true or real... but was it?

Ayah Sakeenah Kalam (8)
Redbridge Primary School, Redbridge

THE HOUSE

Amanda went out in the spooky night trick or treating. She stumbled on a house. This was the best-decorated house but why was it here?
Bang! Bang! The door opened.
"Trick or treat?" I shouted.
No one was there. Should I go in? I stumbled on a disgusting bedroom. I tripped and opened the closet when I looked up, I saw a witch. Was it a costume? If it was, it was amazing. It had a huge, disgusting pimple. Was that real? I didn't think it was real.

Aiza Dossul (8)
Redbridge Primary School, Redbridge

THE HOUSE OF DEATH

It was midnight, there wasn't any light, it was all darkness. I felt something, I felt like running but I couldn't go! The wind swirled around me, warning, "Beware, beware, don't come inside!" I had to go. I walked towards the door and the door opened. I entered the kitchen. Slowly, I pushed the fridge and saw a jar of eyeballs and rotten flesh. I closed the fridge, then I ended up in a blue room with no door with a deadly, blue baby with a knife...

Afaaf Hamid (9)
Redbridge Primary School, Redbridge

THE WOLF CHASE

Terrified, I ran speedily into the ramshackle, misty, broken down woods. A thing was chasing me with a bird on his shoulder. It was dark. I couldn't see but he ran out of it. He got his sharp claws out, ready to attack me. His mask fell off - it was Dad! He told me he was looking for a wolf. Then, out of nowhere, the roar of an animal was nearby. Me and my dad ran, the wolf caught up so we tried not to make a sound. The wolf got his claws out, ready to attack us...

Yusuf Taher (8)
Redbridge Primary School, Redbridge

THE FORBIDDEN WOOD

It was dark. I walked along the path. I felt people watching me. I felt so horrified and unsafe! I went through an archway with ravens nesting on top.
In the distance, I heard a voice say, "Hello, Hannah, why are you here?"
I tried to scream but nothing came out! A vampire swooped me up and was about to bite me for his tea. With a quick think, I was in chains. I had an idea to get free. I painfully took a knife and cut the chains and ran back home.

Imaan Zahra Peerbaccus (8)
Redbridge Primary School, Redbridge

VAMPIRE DOOM

I entered the house. All was dark. I found a
light switch and pressed it. I saw a staircase
and went up it. I spotted an interesting room,
so I went inside!
When I went inside, it was boring so I turned
around to leave but the door was locked! I
turned around and saw a vampire! She tied me
up and put my bag next to me! I found a knife
in my bag so I cut the rope. I suddenly found a
secret door so I ran out. Daylight at long last!

Muzn Hassan (8)
Redbridge Primary School, Redbridge

THE HOUSE OF HORROR

On the way back from university, Eric saw a huge, terrifying house as big as a giant dinosaur. He approached the house to open the oak door. As he went into the house, suddenly he fell into a dungeon. He was surrounded. Eric tried to escape but he couldn't get out, the cats were so bloodthirsty they roared and pounced as quick as lightning...

Danyal Tufael Ahmed (8)
Redbridge Primary School, Redbridge

YOU HAVE TO SEE IT TO BELIEVE IT

Once, someone was putting her daughter to bed when she asked, "Are monsters real?"
Mum replied, "No!" and left.
Later, she heard a scream. She rushed into the bedroom, finding her daughter sitting on the bed.
Mum sighed, "Monsters aren't real!"
Her daughter whispered, "They are."
Mum didn't hear. She walked to the wardrobe and her daughter was there.
She said, "Mummy, there's something in my bed."
Mum took a step and saw what looked like her, crying.
She croaked, "Mummy, why?"
As she said that, her face contorted into eyes with black holes.
She whispered, "You were my favourite..."

Nuala Elsie Hedges (10)
Roxwell CE (VC) Primary School, Roxwell

THE GIRL IN THE GRAVEYARD

'Twas twilight on Halloween, every human soul was resting. All except for one brave character, Katie, who was the most mischievous child in the neighbourhood! *Crash!* A flash of lightning struck the sky, stabbing the radiant moon. She crept through the abandoned graveyard which was so spine-chilling that it would make Dracula's fangs drop out!

"Come play with me," echoed around.

"Arghh! Help!"

Trees grasped out to grab her, voices of a girl echoed inside her head. Katie was not alone. *Boom!* A flash of light, then darkness rapidly revealed the silhouette of the little girl that haunted her...

Emily Iszatt (11)
Roxwell CE (VC) Primary School, Roxwell

COUNT CHEESTRINGULA

One cheesy night, Chalbert the cheese king was wandering around his crowded cheese palace when he saw that his extraordinary butler was dead! Suddenly, a figure approached the king. It was Count Cheestringula!
Count Cheestringula murdered the king tragically with his lethal fangs. The trees were scarce in Cheesewood but that didn't stop Chemily from advancing through it. Her silhouette danced off the thousands of camouflaged trees. Suddenly, she came face-to-face with the Count himself. Nothing could stop the mass murderer from slaughtering the poor, innocent girl. The Count was unstoppable, he would never stop killing citizens...

Jamie Tweed (10)
Roxwell CE (VC) Primary School, Roxwell

ANNABELL

It was a clear day. There was a coach driving up the drive of the new orphanage. The five girls strolled out with their matron. Then they all ran off to play, apart from the one called Lilly, who broke her leg so used crutches.
She asked the owner in the kitchen, "Where shall I sleep?"
"Sleep upstairs, use your crutch," he replied.
Lilly tried to get upstairs. Suddenly, silence.
Lilly's crutch broke! She fell to her knees. She didn't scream or anything like that.
She just stared at the figure opposite her who said very spookily, "Hello, I'm Annabell!"

Tilly Drakeford (9)
Roxwell CE (VC) Primary School, Roxwell

THE DEADLY HOUSENUALA

She stepped into the house, the door shut behind her. She heard footsteps.
"Arghh!"
Blood trickled down her face.
The next day, she woke up in a strange bed, it felt different. She was very scared because this wasn't normal!
A voice appeared and said, "You are my slave now. I am your master."
She said, "Okay, but why? Why me?"
When he came out from the shadows she discovered he was a vampire! It was so scary, she fainted. The vampire was delighted.
"Ha! Now I can wrap her up in chains and put her in my dungeon!"

Olivia Grace Amelie Maund (9)
Roxwell CE (VC) Primary School, Roxwell

DON'T SCREAM

The door slammed, the wind came through the window. Then it felt like the world froze...
slam! Two bloody hands glued to the wet window, slowly a face rose up and smiled with its yellow pointy teeth and red lava eyes.
"Help!" screamed the little girl under her bed.
Mom ran into her room and the girl was gone. All that was left was a sentence that read in blood: 'Don't scream!'
Meanwhile, outside the window was a dead body that had been eaten. The mom went to close the window in the girl's room. She wondered, *who's the killer?*

Lola Lawrence (9)
Roxwell CE (VC) Primary School, Roxwell

DEEP, DARK AND ALONE

One night, three little kids were alone in the forest. One was called Alex, she was nine. Ben was ten and Charlotte was eleven. They were out fishing when they saw a rustle in the bushes. They screamed and ran but before you knew it, they were tied up, being held hostage.
"Gotcha!"
"Help! Help! Please!" yelled out Ben.
Reaching for his iPhone, he dialled 999.
"Police! Police! Help! There's this guy that's holding me and my sisters hostage!"
The police were there and they got into the room and saw that all the kids were dead.

Lola Mason-Braimah (9)
Roxwell CE (VC) Primary School, Roxwell

THE GIRL WHO PLAYED WITH MADNESS

One eerie and spooky night, a girl called Jolene took a walk in the nearby graveyard. She didn't know it was home to werewolves, vampires and who knows what else!
A zombie started to follow her, it was about the most sinister zombie you could imagine.
She looked behind her. She started to run at breakneck speed. She saw a disembodied head hanging from a tree. She reached the last grave.
Suddenly, a face that looked like a cow said, "I shall hath your soul!"
In an instant, Jolene was dead. This was the end of Jolene.
"Ha!" he said.

Lukas Colese (9)
Roxwell CE (VC) Primary School, Roxwell

GRANNIE

One gloomy night, there was a boy called Ben
and he was struggling down the road but little
did he know, he was walking *away* from home,
not *to* home. The street lights started to flicker.
There was no one in the light office so it
became a problem. The lights didn't stop
flickering until he was in ghost land. All he
could see was his old, old grandma who got
shot for bait in WWI. He never got to see her.
"He! He! He!" the ghosts came closer and
closer.
"Mum! Help!"
No one came...

Reece Carter (10)
Roxwell CE (VC) Primary School, Roxwell

MIDNIGHT MURDER

I was walking down the street with my flashlight. It was a blue moon and suddenly, I got a message. I checked my phone and it said: 'Run!'

I ignored it until I started to hear screams and laughs and then my phone pinged. It said: 'Go! Run!'

I started to run.

When I got home, the door was locked but there was a window open so I climbed through. There was a dead body on the floor, I thought, but then its hand moved. I turned around for one second and the body was gone. There was only blood...

Mya Phillips (10)

Roxwell CE (VC) Primary School, Roxwell

HALLOWEEN

"Trick or treat?" I exclaimed as I collected the sweets and put them in my basket.
"What sweets did you get?" my best friend, Enya, asked as I showed her.
We walked to the houses one by one until we reached the end of the lane. I saw a ghostly house with broken windows. It had a pumpkin on the lawn. We slowly crept forwards, trying hard not to step on the grass. We walked up to the door. I stepped on the stairs and they creaked. Someone opened the door. As I took a closer look, it was Gran!

Daisy Georgina Hedges (10)
Roxwell CE (VC) Primary School, Roxwell

THE HORRIFYING SCHOOL!

A long time ago, me and my friend were just having a brilliant time walking along until a smell came towards us. It was very peculiar, but we just ignored it and carried on walking. Then we saw this huge, black cobwebby school. All it had were scary signs saying: *Do Not Enter!* written in bloody words. It was terrifying but we both walked in as the door creaked with blood running down. I was shaking!
As soon as we walked in, there was blood everywhere...
"Oh my god!"

Ria Jade Longman (10)
Roxwell CE (VC) Primary School, Roxwell

THE TERRIFYING SLEEPOVER

It was the day of the sleepover, me and my friends and the teachers were here. Once everyone had arrived, we decided to play a game of hide-and-seek. I got voted to count. As I went to find everyone, I saw this big shadow in the distance. Then I started to think to myself that it wasn't just us here. Then, when I went into Class Four, there was a dead body with maggots on it. It must have been there a while! Who was the murderer and who would be next to die in the creepy school?

Grace Ivey (10)
Roxwell CE (VC) Primary School, Roxwell

THE SCARY SCHOOL

One night, Bob went into this abandoned school. He had a real fear about what was going to be in there. He went into the school through the back entrance. He opened the door to the school and it fell off its hinges.
Bang!
It kind of scared him but he was okay. He carried on walking. He saw all the classes and even the hall. He went into Class Four and there were cobwebs all over the place. The board, the table and the chairs were all broken, even the floor had moss on...

Bailey Waters (9)
Roxwell CE (VC) Primary School, Roxwell

THE MONSTER PARTY

I am at my new house that is colossal. I go into my room, then I hear music and wolves howling in the attic. I want to go up there to investigate but I also have an urge not to so I wait until the next day.
It's midnight and I hear the music again so I build up the confidence to march up there. The music gets louder and louder until I open the trapdoor and see the craziest sight of all. I see monsters dancing and drinking blood from plastic cups. It is weird and pretty funny!

Hayden Thorneycroft (9)
Roxwell CE (VC) Primary School, Roxwell

THE SCARIEST NIGHT OF MY LIFE!

One day, my friends and I went to a building. I was a bit scared but my friend said he went there the night before so that made me feel safer. As we walked in, we saw blood and dead bodies. I didn't know if it was fake but it was still scary. We walked further but the door shut and wouldn't open. Then we heard a scream and then a man walked in with a knife. We broke the door open and we ran into the forest. One of my friends was too slow and died. I was terrified!

Jade Copping (10)
Roxwell CE (VC) Primary School, Roxwell

LOVE CAN LEAD TO NIGHTMARES

Evlin and Exar were in the woods playing hide-and-seek. They both liked each other but that day, Exar couldn't find Evlin and at that moment, he heard her voice with another.
The voice sounded ghostly, but it said, "Brains!"
Exar turned around.
"Who's there?" he cried.
The voice was there again. It was a mummy!
"Evlin, come out!" Exar screamed.
"Why?" she replied.
Exar was frightened about what had happened to his girlfriend.
"Evlin," he paused, "I love you! Ouch!"
He was pinched.
"Get up, sleepyhead!"
It was Evlin. It was just a dream!

Katie Preou (10)
Stifford Clays Primary School, Stifford Clays

DEAR DRACULA

Standing in front of Dracula's castle, Luna convinced her friend it was a fake castle. As night began, with daytime clothes still on, it was time... Trembling with fear, Midnight opened the castle door with excited Luna behind her. Suddenly, there was a big bang of the creaking door. Midnight pounded on the hard, wooden door.

"Don't be such a baby!" whispered Luna a little too loudly.

"Did I hear a human with blood?" came a voice.

"Let us out!" yelled Midnight.

"No!" he said.

The thing appeared. The door opened, Luna escaped. Midnight fell to the floor and died...

Jessica Witterick (10)
Stifford Clays Primary School, Stifford Clays

THE HAUNTED HOTEL

There was a family that wanted to go on vacation. A spooky one of course! It was Halloween. They all wanted to go to the haunted hotel, all full of fun! They packed their bags and set off. They drove in a small, red car. They all arrived at the hotel. The mum heard whispering voices. Suddenly, a door opened. There was a creaking sound from inside. The dad went in the hotel.
"Anyone here?"
There was a voice.
"We're here!"
The rest of the family followed inside.
Mr Vampire said, "We're here!"
Everyone was scared and screamed, "Arghh!"

Amina Seedat (7)
Stifford Clays Primary School, Stifford Clays

THE MAGIC PORTAL

Zack and Callum went trick or treating.
Afterwards, Zack asked, "How about we go to my house?"
"Okay," replied Callum.
They went to Zack's house. When they got there, it looked strange but they went in anyway. They didn't see the sign that said: *Haunted House* written in blood.
When Zack and Callum went in they saw a magic portal and went in.
On the other side, it was dark and misty. They could even hear creepy ghost spirits. All of a sudden, a headless man with bloody claws absorbed the ghost spirits then attacked them, why was this happening?

Theodora Faniyi (9)
Stifford Clays Primary School, Stifford Clays

TRICK OR TREAT?

On a cold Halloween night, Lilly and her friends went trick or treating.
After about an hour, they ended up in the old, creepy forest and saw the abandoned house of Lilly's ancestor.
"Give us sweets!" her friend shouted.

The door creaked open slowly and Lilly bravely walked in. Without thinking, she walked around and went upstairs. She noticed a trail of blood and followed it without looking up. When she did, she saw a ghost of a girl with long hair and a white dress stained with blood. Lilly ran and ran without breathing, then she accidentally tripped...

Scarlet Maddox (10)
Stifford Clays Primary School, Stifford Clays

MARTIN'S CREEPY DREAM IN A DESERT!

Martin was in a dry desert walking slowly and weirdly, no one was in sight. Martin felt lonely. Suddenly, straight after he ran over the creepiest, highest hill, giant zombies and pale, ugly and horrid mummies appeared everywhere! Martin was so shocked he couldn't move a tiny inch! Something was stopping him. He turned around as slow as a slug. What was it? It was the king zombie! Well, Martin thought it was one. The desert was massive and there wasn't an escape here!
Martin whispered, "It's time for *death!*"
What next? Then he woke up...

Alice Watts (7)
Stifford Clays Primary School, Stifford Clays

THE WOLF BOY

A young boy, Luke, moved into Scream Street.
One dark night, Luke struggled to sleep and then hair rose out of his skin and he turned into a wolf! He killed his own parents!
Luke went out to people's houses and killed everybody, leaving scrapes on the sofa, blood on the windows.
The next morning, Luke found himself in the middle of the road and saw nobody.
"What happened?" questioned Luke. "Why's there a massive shadow in front of me?"
It was a clown, blood dripping out of his eyes.
It was a dream. Luke was back in his home.

Jaden Kurdo Shekhbizeny (7)
Stifford Clays Primary School, Stifford Clays

ON HALLOWEEN NIGHT

One spooky Halloween night, four best friends called Annabel, Millie, Sophia and Ella went trick or treating and something spooky popped up behind them. They didn't know what it was! They saw really sharp thorns on the top of spooky heads. They felt petrified! They ran around the corner screaming, but then the spookiest thing happened - a zombie appeared out of nowhere!
The best friends, Annabel, Millie, Sophia and Ella, went to Mrs Dessoy's house but then no one was home so they asked them their names. They were their friends dressed up spookily!

Annabel Jean Butterfield (8)
Stifford Clays Primary School, Stifford Clays

THE WHISPERING SHADOW MAN

There was an abandoned house in the woods.
Inside were whispers of an old shadow man
that whispered in your ear when you went
near. Jonathan was once roaming the woods
and discovered the very same house that
haunted him ever since he was whispered at.
A dark shadow appeared in front of him but his
face glowed with his smile, growing wider until
it was big enough to swallow him whole.
Then he shouted in Jonathan's ear, "Get out of
my house, you little rat!"
Finally, he dragged Jonathan upstairs and
threw him out of a broken window.

Harry Mason (10)
Stifford Clays Primary School, Stifford Clays

THE DISCO

The air was heavy, a thick fog fell over the buildings. Benny was a rebellious teenager who was listening to the music across the road. He lived near the social club that was having their annual disco, although his mother felt strongly concerned about the disco, so he couldn't go. The music grew louder as it came closer. Benny peered out of his window and couldn't believe what he saw. He jumped out of his window to greet his family, all holding speakers, on their way home. He instantly jumped back in shock. They were all different, they were zombies!

Melissa McDonald (10)
Stifford Clays Primary School, Stifford Clays

BACKWARD BOOK

On Tuesday, at Spooky Sagas School, Zoe, who was eight, went to the library to get out her favourite book called 'Little Red Riding Hood'. This would be the twelfth time she had read it! Without hesitation, she opened it but to her shock, this time was different, *very* different. All the words were printed out backwards and were about Zoe getting eaten by a werewolf. This was already very freaky so she started to scream.
The next thing she knew, she was lying down on her bed. *I never knew dreams could feel so real*, thought Zoe.

Katie Webster (10)
Stifford Clays Primary School, Stifford Clays

THE MAD MAN

It was nearly Halloween. Elizabeth Jones was out in the woods when she met him. His eyes were redder than blood, his ears were sharper than a needle, his teeth were a thousand knives. His smile was longer than a sausage dog and he just glanced at her.
"Night," he said as he slowly put her to sleep.

Eighteen hours later, she woke. Elizabeth was petrified! The man carved a message in her arm, it said: *EJ49*. He threw her into a cell with other people that looked just like her.
She slowly woke. Thank goodness it was a dream!

Mackenzie Redding (11)
Stifford Clays Primary School, Stifford Clays

THE MYSTERIOUS WEREWOLF

Charlie and his dog were outside playing and they were looking at the red moon. They suddenly heard a werewolf's howl. They ran away to the park but were followed, it wouldn't leave them alone! Max, the puppy, fled into the bushes. It went deeper, then something bad happened. The werewolf grabbed the dog. He could hear him barking.
In the distance, he noticed the werewolf's footprints. It led to a house. Charlie barged in and saw Max! He grabbed him and ran home. Since that day, Max changed. An evil spirit was growing inside of him...

Thomas Mason (10)
Stifford Clays Primary School, Stifford Clays

ZOMBIES

It was a dark and stormy night when it happened.
Thousands of years later, there were some kids that were just playing around then their lives turned into a disaster! All because of them messing around in the old, rotten forest. They were playing a game called 'Kill The Zombie'. Suddenly, they were in the middle of the forest, running closer to the cottage that had gone missing hundreds of years before. As quick as a drill, they were searching around the cottage. They found a potion and drunk it and from that night on, they were zombies!

Libby Skinner (10)
Stifford Clays Primary School, Stifford Clays

THE SCARIEST DAY OF MY LIFE

Josh and Olivia were walking to the house they always played in but now it was dark, there was a light flicking so they went in. There was a blood stain on the wall. Their hearts were racing at the time but they carried on walking until there was another stain on the floor! They went upstairs and there was a body, but they were alive, luckily! Olivia and Josh went back to the stains but they were gone. *How strange*, they both thought. There was a knock on the door. Olivia went back to the blood. "It's ketchup!"

Katie Boultwood (10)
Stifford Clays Primary School, Stifford Clays

THE MAN WITH NO FACE

One misty day, Jack was walking his dog, Biscuit, through the forest. *Thud!*
What was that? thought Jack. He turned around to see that Biscuit, his beloved dog, had disappeared.
Jack had been searching for Biscuit for hours but there was no sign of him. Just as Jack was about to give up, he heard a rustle, was it Biscuit or not? It was coming closer and closer until he realised it was Biscuit! Jack ran as fast as he could, which wasn't that fast, until he saw something looking at them both with no face...

George Hirt (10)
Stifford Clays Primary School, Stifford Clays

THE HAUNTED PRISON

A long time ago, there was a sinister prison.
This prison was no ordinary prison, it had zombies in it! They'd haunted the prison for over a hundred years.
There was a man called Joe. He was a prisoner at the prison. He'd been there for ninety years, he was now ninety-nine. He fell asleep quickly but in his sleep, something extremely bad happened... he died.
The next morning, the rest of the prisoners were screaming loudly because there was a zombie! It was old and wrinkly with two eyes that were as dark as night...

Joseph Moore (9)
Stifford Clays Primary School, Stifford Clays

THE DISAPPEARING MAN!

After Chloe had her dinner at the popular beach restaurant she headed home. As she left she noticed a man, black clothes and black hair. She didn't know who he was but he was staring at her, at least she thought so! She looked behind her to see if anyone else was there. There was no one. Just the restaurant and the dark blue sea. Now she was definitely sure the man was looking at her, she turned back... but in the time it took a wave to crash on the shore, he'd disappeared, completely! Where had he gone?... Just where?

Eevee Brennan-Pickett (10)
Stifford Clays Primary School, Stifford Clays

KNOCK DOWN DANGER

It was a Wednesday night at a hotel in Pennsylvania. The lightning struck the dark streets. Bob and Peter were in their room. They couldn't sleep so Bob had an idea to play Knock Down Ginger so Peter picked a door. He knocked three times and ran away. An elderly woman with dark eyes opened the door and laughed. It was quite scary because they didn't know why she laughed. They saw one house with no light, so they went to it.
The door opened. Bob went in, a figure was standing there. Then the door slammed shut...

Arnold Sadomba (11)
Stifford Clays Primary School, Stifford Clays

THE NIGHT-TIME NIGHTMARE!

The cool night breeze whistled softly, blowing lightly through my hair. I could feel the stars smiling down at me. I closed my window to get ready for my slumber. I heard strange whispering underneath my bed so I went to check, and I always say danger is my middle name, so I suddenly got transported to a peculiar place. I spotted a door in the distance. I opened the door and saw an evil, sinister witch standing there with fingers and all sorts of horror. I tried my best to escape this evil witch but it didn't happen...

Laylah-Mae Florence Silvain (10)
Stifford Clays Primary School, Stifford Clays

THE MAN WITH SHARP TEETH

One gloomy day, Bill went trick or treating. His mum told him to be home at 10pm.
Bill said, "Okay!"
He got lots of candy, then he was walking home. He got a bit lost so he carried on walking. He went into a forest, then he stopped. He saw teeth marks. Then Bill heard a twig break behind so he looked back and saw the sharp-teethed man. He ran home as fast as he could before 10pm.
He said, "I'm going to bed!"
He woke up and saw his parents dead on the floor. He saw sharp teeth...

James Richard Webb (10)
Stifford Clays Primary School, Stifford Clays

DP THE THIRD

One night, a boy and girl called Sam and Sophie went goofing around in a cemetery, even though they'd heard rumours of DP (Dayton Prime). They wanted to look for him. They split up east and west, running opposite ways. Knowing if they looked in his eyes, they would be possessed.
A few moments later, Sam heard a loud thump! He looked behind him. It was just a stone falling down. Sam heard a scream and ran to Sophie, she was leaking with blood. Sam looked up at the slightest move. He saw DP, possessed he was...

Ethan Jacoyange (10)
Stifford Clays Primary School, Stifford Clays

THE SINGING DOLL

It was 1905, Polly had been dared by her friends to go to an abandoned house seen in the news about to be knocked down. She didn't want to be a wimp so she went in.
Coming from a room upstairs were banging noises and music. A girl was singing a nursery rhyme! She crept upstairs and the noise became louder. She felt sick. Slowly, she turned the doorknob. The music had become louder. A group of men were demolishing the walls and a doll on a chair was singing. Polly blinked, everything had gone. But where?

Omotola Ogundana (11)
Stifford Clays Primary School, Stifford Clays

HAUNTED

Bella and Immy are out on a cold, stormy night in the streets, trick or treating at every house in sight but are now at the last house - the haunted house!
Bella is seven and Immy is twelve, surprisingly their mum let them go alone. Next thing you know, a scream comes from inside the house. The girls huddle together. Immy lets go of Bella to look round the garden but when she goes back to her sister, she's not there, she's indoors. Immy screams for her sister to come back as she can't get in...

Paige Goldfinch (10)
Stifford Clays Primary School, Stifford Clays

THE BOY THAT WAS HAUNTED

There was a boy called Jack. He was just starting his day like any other day. When he was getting his breakfast, he thought he saw a ghost. Now he was starting to worry! He went to bed to rest. He kept saying, "It's a dream!" Then he was woken up by a breeze. He checked if his windows were open, they weren't. He went back to bed and felt really scared. Jack started to drift off to sleep in his bed. When he woke up, he found himself lying in a barn with chainsaws all around him...

Kai Sleeman (11)
Stifford Clays Primary School, Stifford Clays

THE LEGEND OF ALEX AND THE HOUSE

One dark night, there was a boy called Alex. He lived in a scary house with cobwebs.
One day, he went trick or treating on his own. He was scared! He got some chocolate and sweets. He went past a house and all the lights were off, even the bedroom lights were off. He saw the door and opened it. Suddenly, a picture flew past him. He went into the kitchen and on the table, there was mouldy fruit, then he made a noise. Someone came down the stairs. He grabbed Alex's shoulder and turned him around...

Esme Jarmyn Purvis (8)
Stifford Clays Primary School, Stifford Clays

SMILING DOG

Jack was playing on his phone.
Two hours later, he was sent a picture of a smiling dog. Jack deleted it and went to sleep. Jack woke up and had breakfast, then went to the shop to buy some Mentos. He went home and saw a painting on the wall. Jack threw it away and watched TV.
After he woke up the next day, he had a dream of the smiling dog. Jake went to the doctor to see what was wrong but he said it was nothing. Two weeks later, the smiling dog was really there and killed Jack.

Cristian Zarello Collings (11)
Stifford Clays Primary School, Stifford Clays

THE ABANDONED HOUSE

Once upon a time, I was sleeping in my bed. All of a sudden, I ended up at a creepy abandoned house.

I shouted, "Mum, Dad, where are you?"

I heard a noise upstairs so I went up and the floor was too creaky. I checked in all of the rooms and the doors were really squeaky. There was only one more room left, the bathroom! I quietly opened the door and heard the noise in the shower. There was blood on the floor and I opened up the curtains... it was my dad! All of that for nothing!

Eisvina Kusaite (10)
Stifford Clays Primary School, Stifford Clays

FRIDAY THE 4TH

Belle and Lilly were going to a haunted house party. Belle dressed as a dead devil and Lilly dressed up as a dead cat. Belle and Lilly needed to go to the toilet upstairs.
They went up the stairs and suddenly, they heard a bang! It was like a gunshot. There was blood all up the walls and a plastic gun on the floor. Belle and Lilly went in the dark room.
"Oh my god!"
It was just someone getting changed, and the gunshot, that was just someone bursting a balloon!

Isobel Titterton (10)
Stifford Clays Primary School, Stifford Clays

ALEX AND THE CIRCUS

There Alex was, in the circus. He went outside to get a hot chocolate from the little cafe stand on a break. Alex finally got his hot drink but no one was at the stand serving so he kind of just stole it. Alex took a seat and noticed he was the only one around so he was a little anxious. Alex thought he should just go back into the circus so he did. Right when Alex sat down, at that moment, he somehow teleported to another place. Suddenly, he found himself face-to-face with clowns...

Archie-Peter Jarmyn-Purvis (10)
Stifford Clays Primary School, Stifford Clays

THEME PARK SCARE

I was at a theme park, enjoying the rides. All of a sudden, I went into a queue line thinking it was a ride but I was wrong, it was a scare maze! I hated scare mazes! I was the only one in the line.
I went in. As I went in, there was no one around. It was dark and spooky! As I carried on walking, I saw movement as an actor scared me again.
Eventually, someone else came in the maze and helped me escape. They weren't scared like me. We got out and celebrated together.

Daniel Watson (10)
Stifford Clays Primary School, Stifford Clays

SUPER MONSTER AND THE HAUNTED HOUSE

This is William, these are his friends, Billy and Zak. William is a werewolf, Billy is a bat and Zak is a zombie and they live in a haunted house.
Once, they found a haunted house and they thought they should go in. Then they all found a load of signs saying: *Don't Come In!* William and Billy started to walk back but sneakily, Zak went in and then William and Billy went home. Billy and William lived together in a cave and Zak, well, he never came home.

Owen Marchant (7)
Stifford Clays Primary School, Stifford Clays

THE MYSTERIOUS PERSON!

I was in my bedroom, it was silent. There were no cars outside. Wait, what was that noise? There was something moving. It was coming from... behind me! I looked behind me and there was a light and a person was standing there with a cape on. He or she looked very creepy. I could just make out a streak of blood falling from its mouth. It also had very sharp teeth sticking out of its mouth.
Wait a second... it... it was my brother! Joshua had been to a Halloween party!

Olivia Cannon (7)
Stifford Clays Primary School, Stifford Clays

THE WEREWOLF'S DEN

A little boy called Joe went round his friend's house and Kai, Harry and Mason were there so they went on the Xbox for two hours.
After their time of two hours, they went outside for a challenge. It was pitch-black and it was cold. They started playing football and then they started playing basketball. Joe was the best at it! The boys ran to the back of the garden and then a bush started rattling... It was a werewolf!

Russell Lee Ocuneff (11)
Stifford Clays Primary School, Stifford Clays

THE DARK FOREST

On a dark night in 1995, Jake was walking through a scary forest. Suddenly, a loud shout was heard in the forest. Jake's heart was pumping very fast. He stumbled and then was walking very slowly. When a dark black figure was shown, Jake was so nervous, he couldn't look at it! He ran and then looked behind, the figure was gone. Jake was really scared. Later, he looked and the figure was still gone...

Alex Holland (10)
Stifford Clays Primary School, Stifford Clays

THE NIGHTMARE

One rainy day, I was just looking outside, then I heard someone behind me. I couldn't blink.
Then I fainted!
When I woke up, I was in this strange room. It was like someone was behind me. I went to look, it was a monster!
I ran as fast as I could out of the room. I saw Mila and Ash, my pups.
When we got out, there was a vampire and the vampire sucked my blood!

Ronnie Jordan (7)
Stifford Clays Primary School, Stifford Clays

THE DUNGEON

As I woke from my sleep, I noticed I was in some sort of dungeon. My entire body was tied to a chair with rope. I eventually managed to chew my way out of the rope but as soon as I got out, somebody looked over me. Before I knew it, I was back at my house in my bed with my mum and dad staring at me with fear. Was it a dream? Nobody knows...

Eve Garner (10)
Stifford Clays Primary School, Stifford Clays

CHRISTMAS BEFORE HALLOWEEN

One day, before Halloween, something extraordinary happened. Christmas came early because the elves had bought a new turbo-powered present-making machine that makes the present a thousand times quicker than any elf.

A couple of hours later, Santa Claus was woken with this shocking information. He was worried and sleepy. Suddenly, he leapt out of his bed and he rushed to his telephone. *Gulp!* He had to call The Devil! He nervously told him that Halloween would be cancelled because the elves had made all the presents too quickly.

The Devil responded with, "No!"

Santa put down the telephone.

Dylan Sharp (9)

Wells Park School, Lambourne End

666 YEARS AGO

Many years ago, three best friends, Gemma, Piotr and Daisy were at school chilling in the playground.
All of a sudden, Freddie came over and said, "Have you heard about the abandoned hospital?"
He then set them the challenge that they had to go to the hospital for the night.
That night, they made their way to the hospital.
Suddenly, they heard an awkward noise which made them scream. They were walking down the corridor.
All of a sudden, they noticed bloody footsteps on the floor in front of them which led to the theatre room...

Peter Lacazette (10)
Wells Park School, Lambourne End

THE LAKE!

One night, a boy went to a dark lake for a swim, and that was the biggest mistake ever made. He felt something touch him and he screamed! He got out of the lake fast like the Flash!
When he got home, he told his mum but she didn't believe him.
"I did!" he said. "I did!"
His heart was pounding so fast, it felt like it was about to burst out of his chest. His mum went to look, the monster came back!
Then he woke up and said, "Thank god it was just a dream... or was it?"

Alfie Tommy Parsons (10)
Wells Park School, Lambourne End

THE BLOODSUCKING ZOMBIES

There were three friends at school. They were set the challenge to spend the day and night in the haunted London hospital.
When they went into the abandoned hospital, they looked around and all they saw was blood. All of a sudden, something caught Daisy's eye. It was an arm poking out of a cupboard. She screamed. She tried to run away but an arm seemed to be holding her back. She panicked when she realised it was a zombie!
He ripped her heart out and began to eat it when a door opened...

Rhys Lawn (9)
Wells Park School, Lambourne End

VIRUS, THE NIGHT KILLER

At night, there was a robot who stabbed the brains of children and ripped apart souls. Most of the children in the coastal village were dead but there were three who slept during the day and were awake at night which helped them stay alive.
One night, they fell asleep and the monster came. The children heard him and kicked him out the window.
The next day, the kids were called heroes and grew up to tell the story to their kids and for them to tell their kids and so on...

Jayden Hubbard (10)
Wells Park School, Lambourne End

THE LITTLE SCHOOL OF HORRORS

One cold, dark morning, Miss Baghurst dragged herself out of bed with messy hair and quickly jumped into her car.
As she arrived at school, no one was there! It was as if everyone had disappeared! Weird, yet curious, she went on into the building. What was about to happen was unbelievable. She was hit by a cold, dark figure. She fell to the ground in shock and screamed. She quickly jumped up and ran away as she was terrified. As she ran, she went where she thought was safe...

Riley Sharp (9)
Wells Park School, Lambourne End

YOUNG WRITERS INFORMATION

We hope you have enjoyed reading this book – and that you will continue to in the coming years.

If you're a young writer who enjoys reading and creative writing, or the parent of an enthusiastic poet or story writer, do visit our website **www.youngwriters.co.uk**. Here you will find free competitions, workshops and games, as well as recommended reads, a poetry glossary and our blog. There's lots to keep budding writers motivated to write!

If you would like to order further copies of this book, or any of our other titles, then please give us a call or order via your online account.

Young Writers
Remus House
Coltsfoot Drive
Peterborough
PE2 9BF
(01733) 890066
info@youngwriters.co.uk

Join in the conversation!
Tips, news, giveaways and much more!

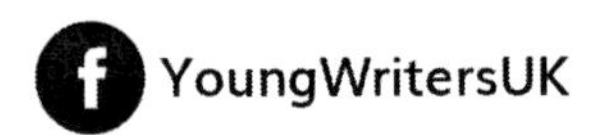

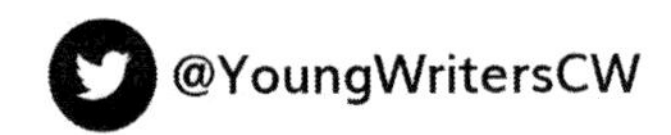